Praise for

"Brutally honest and original...Primamore's work is a complete delight!"
—CRAIG LUCAS, playwright, *An American in Paris.*

"Primamore's plays are superb in their exploration of subject matter, muscular dialogue, and startling stage action."
—HONOR MOLLOY, playwright, *Crackskull Row.*

"Elizabeth Primamore's trio of one acts are a primal scream for old New York values; in the words of her heroine Susan Ponti, 'I am hungry. I wish I had an apple.' Don't we all? In *Just Fine,* Susan asks the question, "Isn't that what places like New York are for? Misfits? Queers? Outcasts?" *Just Fine* decors the apple with one New Yorker's despair, loss, revenge, and leveling the playing field. *Blank* brings us dead center in a passionate ill-fated lesbian relationship between a baby-boomer and a millennial. 'In my day gay marriage was an oxymoron,' Min soliloquizes. Therein lies the rub. The generation gap becomes a full-on fault line as the earth rips open beneath them. In *The Child's Best Interest,* the trio of divorcing parents and their mediator becomes a Bermuda Triangle we're not sure who will survive and who will get sucked under. Each of these plays leaves casualties and pinpoints the time and place of a New York in spiritual crisis. Primamore's are intelligent voices tinged with irony and self-awareness even in the moment the cosmic baby bottle of milk is ripped out of their mouths.
—ANNIE LANZILLOTTO, author of *Hard Candy: caregiving, mourning, and stagelight,* Guernica Editions, 2018.

"Whether it's dealing with the bitter tug of war that's child custody, the slippery love of an Older and Younger woman or the rambling misdirection of a College Professor charged with murder, Elizabeth Primamore is able to share the humanity of her characters and her own heart."
—MARK ST. GERMAIN, playwright, *Freud's Last Session.*

# SHADY WOMEN
## THREE SHORT PLAYS

# SHADY WOMEN

## THREE SHORT PLAYS

**ELIZABETH PRIMAMORE**

Upper Hand
**PRESS**

ISBN: 978-0-9984906-7-0

*Just Fine* first appeared in *Literature and Gender,* Pearson Publishing, 2011.

Cover and interior design by Stewart A. Williams
The typeface used for the text is Italian Old Style MT, based on a design by William Morris from 1911.

Upper Hand Press
P.O. Box 91179
Bexley, Ohio 43209
U.S.A.
https://upperhandpress.com

*To the Memory of Angela J. Costa*
*The Finest Poet I Ever Knew*
*Who Made Life Wondrous*
*With Love*

# CONTENTS

Introduction ................................. 1

*Just Fine* ........................................ 3

*The Child's Best Interest* ......................... 9

*Blank* .......................................... 27

Acknowledgments ......................... 45

About Elizabeth Primamore ............. 47

# INTRODUCTION

*by Joseph Goodrich*

The women—and the men—you'll meet in the following pages are in the worst kinds of trouble. Caught between what they want and what they have, trapped between the past and the present, all they can do is speak.

Look at Susan Ponti in *Just Fine*. Suspected of a capital crime, she finds herself in a police station. A story of love lost and revenge taken spills from a broken heart. We are her interrogators…or her witnesses. One thing is certain: no one's judgment will be harsher than her own. Whether or not she goes to jail, Susan will never be free again.

Gordon and Heather, the couple in *The Child's Best Interest*, gouge each other with fragments of their shared past. They're getting a divorce, and the fate of their child hangs in the balance. Old wounds are opened and older secrets are revealed. This is the most naturalistic of the three plays, shocking in its bursts of physical, verbal, and psychic violence.

*Blank* is a new contribution to a staple of the American one-act: the park bench play. (Albee's *The Zoo Story* is the granddaddy of them all. Mamet's *Duck Variations* also comes to mind.) Primamore puts a spin on the form, mixing the real and the imaginary to capture the end of a relationship.

That's what all three plays are about, really—the end of a

relationship. Whatever the cause—death, cruelty, jealousy—Primamore's characters are alone. Not to be a part of something, not to share a life with someone is to be marked out as different. And, as *Blank*'s Wilhelmina Isabel Brewster observes, "when you're different...life is harder."

To speak is, perhaps, to be heard. The characters in these plays are speaking.

Listen.

JOSEPH GOODRICH is a playwright and the author of *People in A Magazine: S.N. Behrman and The New Yorker* (University of Massachusetts Press, 2018).

# JUST FINE

"Just Fine" (originally titled "questioning") was produced by HB Playwrights Theater, New York City, as part of The Waiting Room Ten Minute Play Festival, 2008. Directed by Rochelle Oliver. Cast: Susan Ponti—Gordana Rashovich.

"Just Fine" is published in *Literature and Gender* (Pearson, 2011) and *New America* (Autumn House Press, 2013).

## CHARACTERS

SUSAN PONTI: Forties. A professional woman with a confident demeanor.

## SETTING

A room in a police station.

## TIME

2008.

(*Susan faces the audience.*)

SUSAN

I did nothing. If I did, wouldn't I be handcuffed? I'm not drunk. Forget smoking pot. You get arrested for that. In my day you could toke in the street—8th Street in the Village—and the cops would walk right past you. Back home we'd ride in the Cadillac. Driving round and round aimlessly. Even high, Jersey was boring. (*Beat*) That cop eyeballing me. I am so sick and tired of people looking at me. Everywhere I go. Even in this filthy shit hole. Diana, get me out of here! She was doing just fine. I know this is about that white coat who calls himself a doctor.

I am not answering any questions without my attorney. I may not know much about what happens in places like this, but I do watch *Law and Order*. Never say a word without a lawyer present. Even if you're innocent. Look what happened to Martha Stewart. Our mouths hung open when we heard the jury's verdict. A woman's luck. (*She looks up.*) You should've seen what happened to Hilary.

I don't look at anyone anymore. When I see people I know coming my way, I try as hard as I can to avoid them. Before Diana died—we'd walk in our neighborhood, and I would say "hi" to everybody. Diana would say to me, "Who are you? The mayor of Tribeca?" Things were so different then.

I am too young to be a widow. But that's what I am.

Even babies in baby carriages stare at me. All over Greenwich Street. Here we are, two artists alien in our own neighborhood. Isn't that what places like New York are for? Misfits? Queers? Outcasts? Now we got battalions of baby carriages. Just like the suburbs we escaped. I'm not talking one or two here. That would be cute. I am talking zillions. Looking at me. (*Beat*) Like the way those nurses looked at us. No one wants to be pitied. Not even the dying.

Where is my bag? A woman needs to know where her pocketbook is. (*Beat*) I'm going on and on here. Where is he? Where is my attorney? (*Beat*) Where are you, bitch?

I know what people whisper to their wives and husbands and significant others or whatever you call them today—there she is, poor thing.

This has got to be the day my lawyer is tied up in court. (*Beat*) You were doing just fine.

If it were up to me, I'd never see anyone again. Ever. Not my mother, my father, my brother, the kids, friends, students. Too many people care about me. What a burden. People caring about you. That's how Diana must've felt. Burdened. Burdened by me.

We were so happy. Still in the prime of our destinies. Together for twenty-five years. With support from no one. We didn't care. (*Beat*) She was doing just fine. This waiting is excruciating. I'd rather be at work.

College teaching is my line.

I was sitting at my desk eating an apple when my phone rings. This is Detective So-and-So. I almost choked. Who? What? Precinct? As in police? Something about a doctor. They think I saw something.

He said if I don't come in for questioning that they would come and get me. I left the half-eaten apple on my desk. Glistening with saliva.

The doctor they want me to tell them about? He was in his seventies and—I'm so thirsty. Officer, can I please have—?

I can't have anything I want. Not even a glass of water. (*Beat*) Everything's killing us. Doctors are killing us, too. I'm not saying they're all terrible. But some of them? Look out! I know because you told me, Diana.

She was doing just fine. Nobody could tell she had cancer. She looked like a regular person. This big shot oncologist everybody's praising to high heavens, cajoled her—like Satan tempted Eve with the apple in the garden of Eden. Except our fall wasn't so fortunate. Diana begged him to fractionate the chemotherapy, but he said "no." Why didn't you insist on it, Diana?

It was downhill from there. The patient knows more than one thinks—we were lying in bed and she looked at me with those rich blue eyes and said, "I hope Doctor So-and-So dies so he'll know what he did to me." I was stunned. I didn't know what she meant then, but I do now.

I hate that place! Hospitals. Lethal memories. But I had no choice the other night. The library I use is near there. That's why I went—

I did see something. He was murdered. The doctor. That doctor. Her doctor. Someone—I don't know who—walked up real close to him as he was leaving the hospital. Suddenly he was lying on the ground, bleeding. His smug expression dissipating into thin air. I saw this big man running—credit cards strewn all over the sidewalk.

I ran the other way. The stones on my vintage bag?

(*She holds up the bag.*)

## SUSAN
These gems refracted the streetlight into some guy's video—somehow, through lots of questioning, photos, and computers, they found me. It must've been the receptionist who gave them the tip because she—the pretty Hispanic girl—knows where I teach. She has the diamond cheek piercing.

(*She points to her cheek.*)

## SUSAN
The kids call it the Marilyn Monroe. When Diana and I would go for her treatments, that cute, little receptionist always commented on my vintage bag. (Beat) He was killed. So what! Why should this bastard walk around and enjoy his children

and grandchildren—the bastard wouldn't listen. (*Looks up.*) Diana, all I wanted was you. Help me, Diana!

It wasn't the gems on my bag here that reflected the light. It was a big, shiny knife that I carried inside of my bag. I took the knife and drove it into his back real hard—and I twisted and twisted it. When I saw blood spurting, I tossed the knife into the sewer. He stumbled, his wallet fell out of his pocket. I kicked it with my high heels. A big guy was walking by and when he heard the doctor scream, he ran. I wanted to level the playing field.

Could I really do something like that? I'm a professor. Not a murderer. But I always wanted to be an actor. Diana thought I'd be great.

I have to go now. My attorney. (*Beat*) I'm hungry. I wish I had an apple.

(*Susan leaves.*)

*END OF PLAY*

# THE CHILD'S BEST INTEREST

"The Child's Best Interest" was produced by HB Playwrights Theater, New York City, as part of The Office Plays Festival, 2014. Directed by Amy Wright.

*Cast:* Gordon Gibson—Nick DeSimone; Heather Fielding—Jen Danby; Jeffrey Singer—Bryon O'Hanlon.

## CHARACTERS

GORDON GIBSON: Thirties, male lawyer.
HEATHER FIELDING: Twenties, teacher's aide, Gordon's wife.
JEFFREY SINGER: Twenty, intern social worker.

## SETTING

An office in a family mediation institute. Desk. Two chairs. Sofa.

## TIME

Afternoon. Present time.

(*GORDON GIBSON, in a black suit, sits. JEFFREY SINGER, in casual Friday clothes, sporting a clipboard, enters.*)

JEFFREY
Hello. My name is Jeffrey Singer.
(*Jeffrey extends his hand. Gordon does not take it.*)

GORDON
Just how long is this stupid meeting going to take?
When's the counselor coming?

JEFFREY
I am the counselor.

(*HEATHER FIELDING enters.*)

HEATHER
I'm sorry I'm late. Hello Gordon.

JEFFREY
Jeffrey Singer. Nice to meet you.

HEATHER
Likewise.

JEFFREY
Thank you both for coming in today. I know this
is a difficult time—
(*Gordon waves his hand as if to say, "cut to the chase."*)

JEFFREY
Alright, Mr. Gibson . . . Not a problem . . .
Uhm . . . We're here today—We're here today because the court—the court ordered me—uhh . . .
mediation to try to settle a custody dispute. It's

part of—the dispute, I mean is part of divorce proceedings between you, Mr. Gibson and you, Ms. Fielding—

HEATHER

Heather, please—

JEFFREY

Pardon me?

HEATHER

Call me Heather—

JEFFREY

Well ... Uhm ... It's not really—Okay, Heather ... To continue, at the center of this dispute is your eight year old son, Jake. Ms.—sorry Heather, is proposing primary custody with reasonable and limited—sorry—limited—I mean unlimited visitation. And Mr. Gibson is proposing joint—

GORDON

This is a waste of my time. There will be no mediation. We will go to trial. (*To Heather*) And then you'll see what you get. (*To Jeffrey*) She thinks because she's getting her happy little divorce that she can get my son, too. Put that in your official file, Mr. Counselor.

JEFFREY

My name—

HEATHER

At least give him the courtesy to finish, Gordon.

JEFFREY
Mr. Gibson, you propose joint physical custody.

GORDON
The only way my son has a chance at a successful
future is by living with me.

JEFFREY
How is that, Mr. Gibson?

GORDON
Do you believe in academic achievement? Hard
work? Discipline? High expectations? Literature?
Art? Music?

JEFFREY
Sure.

HEATHER
Try love and understanding, Gordon, or don't
those things matter?

GORDON
There you go with your hippie bull again.

JEFFREY
Excuse me? You both understand that the court
considers a number of factors that would serve the
child's best interest. Emotional security counts.

GORDON
What are you saying? I don't love my son?

JEFFREY
No, no.

GORDON

Are you saying I don't love my son?

JEFFREY

No, not at all.

GORDON

Would I be sitting—

HEATHER

Gordon, please. You blow everything out of proportion.

GORDON

Would I be sitting through this bull crap mediation if I didn't love my son?

HEATHER

You made your point. The man is trying to do his job.

JEFFREY

What do you do for a living, Heather?

HEATHER

I'm a teacher's aide. Elementary school.

GORDON

Isn't that in your file?

JEFFREY

What's that—oh, yes, I forgot. Sorry—you're my first—never mind.

HEATHER

I remember my first day at my job. It's both ex-
hilarating and scary. You're doing alright, Jeffrey.
Any mother would be proud.

JEFFREY

Thanks.

GORDON

America's got no talent.

HEATHER

As wonderful a father as Mr. Gibson is, I think
our son would be better off living with me, who
gets home from work at three instead of midnight.
Who's home on weekends and holidays. I don't
want my son calling nannies "mommy."

GORDON

She says she doesn't want Jake to call strangers
"mommy." (*To Heather.*) Well, when Jake spends
too much time with you, he ends up treating me
like a stranger.

HEATHER

You're never around.

GORDON

Do you know who I am, Mr. Counselor?

JEFFREY

My name sir, is Jef—

GORDON

Do you know who I am? I am one of the most re-
spected and feared litigation attorneys in the state.

JEFFREY

Wow.


GORDON

Looking forward to facing me in court?


JEFFREY

I thought we were going to try here—Mr. Gibson, I do understand how much you care about your son, but Heather's offer seems quite workable for the two of you with your client obligations. Your grueling work schedule.


GORDON

I work sixteen-hour days and every other weekend, for Jake's sake.


HEATHER

So do I. Making after school arrangements. Seeing to Jake's doctor appointments. Preparing his favorite meals.


GORDON

Watching TV. Playing board games. Cards. Before you know it, he's acting like I don't know who, instead of my son.


HEATHER

You do exaggerate, Gordon. We have fun together.


GORDON

And who do you think pays for all of this fun?


(*Gordon's phone rings.*)

GORDON

The big house? The jaguar? The finest private schools? Who? Huh? You?

(*Answers phone.*)

GORDON

Hello.

(*Loses call.*)

HEATHER

I appreciate the wonderful life you've given us, Gordon.

GORDON

Now do you understand, Mr. Counselor? Why I worry about my son having a functional brain?

JEFFREY

My name sir, is Jeffrey—

GORDON

And how that will be impossible if he continues to live with this floozy who calls herself a mother? (*Heather's phone rings.*)

HEATHER

That's not fair, Gordon. Excuse me.

(*Has trouble finding phone in her bags. Finds it. Answers phone.*)

HEATHER

Hello. Let me talk to him. Your tummy hurts? Mommy will be home soon, okay? Yes, daddy's here.

(*Gordon walks toward Heather.*)

JEFFREY
(*Overlapping as Gordon approaches Heather.*)

Sir ... Sir.

HEATHER
Not now, honey. He's—Mommy and Daddy are
busy. Everything is going to be okay. I—don't cry,
be a big boy. Have a glass of milk.

(*Hangs up.*)

GORDON
Jake wanted to talk to me.

HEATHER
His stomach is bothering him again.

JEFFREY
Please, let's try—mine, too.

HEATHER
We've got to stop arguing in front of him. (*Beat*)
Years ago. When we were first married. I was
young. You were away so much, leaving me—I was
lonely. Confused. I made a mistake.

GORDON
With the Shop Rite assistant store manager. I ran
him out of town like a yellow belly hyena.

HEATHER
You're no forty-year old virgin.

GORDON

I hope not.

HEATHER

You know what I mean. That prostitute.

GORDON

She was a high class call girl. Five grand an hour. Bunch of guys at a bachelor party.

JEFFREY

Please, please. None of this does anything to serve Jake's best interest. He just called you. Upset.

HEATHER

I'm sorry.

JEFFREY

May I ask, why did the two of you stay together if things were rocky from the beginning?

HEATHER

You stayed to save face in front of your family. When I married him I knew he was the one, or so I thought. We had so much fun together. He was so suave and charming. Reciting poetry . . .

GORDON

"She walked in beauty like the night/Climes and starry skies/And all that's best of dark and bright/ Met in her aspect and her eyes." Byron . . . And now.

HEATHER

And now . . . Heaven turned to hell.

JEFFREY

Just a minute—

GORDON

That's what I get for thinking with the wrong head. You know, I've had enough of this mediation bull. Guess what? Now I'm going to sue you for sole physical custody.

JEFFREY

You can do that, sir, but usually the court favors the primary caretaker.

GORDON

Unless—

JEFFREY

And from what I understand—

GORDON

Unless I prove the primary caretaker unfit.

HEATHER

Oh, Christ.

JEFFREY

Would you really want to do that?

GORDON

Why wouldn't I?

JEFFREY

That wouldn't be in your son's best interest.

GORDON

It would prove I'm the better parent.

HEATHER

Gordon, please be reasonable.

GORDON

With a little help from my friends I will alienate you from the court-appointed psychiatrist, Jake's teachers, and the parents of his playmates.

HEATHER

I'll block you from decision making and tell Jake his father is a real drag!

GORDON

I'll hire experts to convince the court that I am the better parent.

HEATHER

Whatever.

GORDON

Whatever? Experts are very, very expensive. She doesn't stand a chance, Mr. Counselor.

JEFFREY

My name is Jeffrey Singer.

GORDON

Singer, huh? Well, my boy, see her? You're looking at an irresponsible, sexually immoral and undisciplined woman. My parenting skills, on the other hand, are rock steady. So good luck to the both of you.

HEATHER

I'm not going to let you get away with this.

GORDON

Watch me.

JEFFREY

We can try—

HEATHER

Gordon, wait, think for a minute—

JEFFREY

We can try one more time. After you've cooled your jets.

HEATHER

Our son loves the both of us. You know what. I'll agree to joint physical custody.

GORDON

Too late.

JEFFREY

You're getting what you want, Mr. Gibson.

GORDON

Not anymore.

HEATHER

But I'm agreeing . . . You're never satisfied. What about Jake?

GORDON

What about Jake?

JEFFREY

Yes, what him? The boy? The innocent son?

**HEATHER**
Well, you might not like it, but I'm his mother.

**GORDON**
And you might not like it, but I'm his father.

**HEATHER**
You're—

**JEFFREY**
Please calm, down. The two of you—

**GORDON**
Merrily we go to trial.

**HEATHER**
No you're not, Gordon.

**GORDON**
Yes, we are. Then you'll see what you get.

**HEATHER**
That's not what I meant. You're not—you're not Jake's father, Gordon.

**GORDON**
I'm not what?

**HEATHER**
Jake's father. You're not his biological father.

**GORDON**
Hah! Look at the extent she'll go to. Pathetic tactic, isn't it?

### HEATHER
It's not a tactic.

### JEFFREY
Oh God.

### GORDON
In my business, I've seen and heard every trick in the book.

### HEATHER
You were away. It happened.

### JEFFREY
Oh, dear God. My God. My God. I'm just a kid. A kid. I'm just a little kid.

### GORDON
Oh really?

### HEATHER
I had a prenatal paternity test because I wasn't sure—

### GORDON
Yeah right. Let's see the evidence.

### JEFFREY
A prenatal paternity test ...

### HEATHER
Alright.

(*Heather hands Gordon the document. He reads it.*)

### GORDON

My whole life has been a lie? And what about
Jake's? Huh? Did you ever think of him?

(*Jeffrey pours himself a glass of milk.*)

### HEATHER

Jake loves you.

### GORDON

I don't believe this.

(*Stunned for a minute, then lunges for her.*)

### GORDON

I'll kill you. You selfish monster.

### HEATHER

Don't touch me. Get away!

### GORDON

Whore! Bitch! With my bare hands I'll strangle
you.

### JEFFREY

Hey! Hey!

(*As Jeffrey breaks them apart, Heather runs out. Gordon collapses in
chair.*)

### JEFFREY

Mr. Gibson? Mr. Gibson?

(*Jeffrey gets Gordon a glass of water.*)

### JEFFREY
Sir?

### GORDON
Gordon ...

### JEFFREY
What's that?

### GORDON
Call me Gordon.

### JEFFREY
Mr. Gibson? Are you sure?

### GORDON
Please, Gordon.

### JEFFREY
Gordon, sir, when you think about it, you know—
you know that you're the only father Jake has ever
known.

(*Gordon puts his arm around Jeffrey.*)

### GORDON
Yeah.

## END OF PLAY

# BLANK

"Blank" was produced by HB Playwrights Theatre, New York City, as part of The Central Park Plays Festival, 2015. Directed by Lyto Triantafyllidou. Cast: Wilhelmina Isabel Brewster—Paula O'Brien; Girl—Amanda Schussel.

## CHARACTERS

WILHELMINA ISABEL BREWSTER: Fifties-sixties, baby boomer "slacker."
GIRL: Late teens, a young woman, millennial.

## SETTING

Stage is bare except for a park bench. A canvas bag is on the bench.

## TIME

Present.

(*The song "Oh My Heart"\* plays. MIN enters. She's wearing casual clothes and black eyeliner. She's holding drum sticks.*)

### MIN

One-eanda-two-eanda-three-eanda  Da.  One-eanda-two-eanda-three  eanda  Da.  One-eanda-two-eanda-three-eanda. (switches to quarter note triplets) Da-da-da. Da-da-da. Da-da- (*Beat*) Ta da!

(*She bows, hums the first line of "Here Comes the Bride," and sits down on the bench. She puts the sticks down.*)

### MIN

Beautiful day, isn't it? Good a day as any to—my name is Min. Short for Wilhelmina. Been called Min since a kid. Even though I didn't like it ... Or maybe I did like it. Anyway, the name Min stuck. Like a stalled train.

Then I landed this part-time job. With my brother's help. It's a—you know, W2, paycheck kind of job. Never done that before. A gig here. A gig there. That's fine with me. What's so great about ambition anyway? Look where it got Caesar.

(*Min bats her eyes, which catch a little dirt or piece of leaf. She rubs that away. Her eyeliner smudges.*)

### MIN

Sandro—that's my nephew—he laughs when this happens. I'm so happy to see him smile because when you're different, like going it alone, life is harder.

So anyway, at work ... This child—

(*GIRL enters.*)

MIN
While I was putting on my hair net.

(*Sound of dance music. They dance. Continues speaking to audience.*)

GIRL
Slipped it in.

MIN
White pockets flapping.

GIRL
I heard the beat of the toms.

MIN
She just showed up.

GIRL
That night my body.

MIN
At a gig.

GIRL
Had a mind of its own.

MIN
A budding artist like San, but this ...

(*The music stops. They stop dancing, face each other.*)

MIN
Do you know how old I am ?

GIRL

Forty-five? Fifty?

MIN

Keep going.

GIRL

So?

(*To the Audience.*)

MIN

It was only coffee.

GIRL

And the Coney Island Aquarium.

MIN

The Bronx Zoo.

GIRL

A drum lesson in Central Park.

MIN

Under the weeping willow tree.

GIRL

Willow.

MIN

She called me Willow.

GIRL

It was . . .

### MIN
Crazy ... I couldn't help it.

(*The Girl leaves.*)
(*Min's cell phone chirps. She reads the text.*)

### MIN
That was two years ago. And yeah, things are a little rocky sometimes like with anything. My brother's cool with it. And there's Sandro thank goodness, with the guitars and video games. A real family.

God, this feels weird. Know what I mean? In my day gay marriage was an oxymoron. An impossibility. Sometimes I want to kill the U.S. Supreme Court. Who needs all this pressure? I liked being an outsider. My girlfriend—I know she's young, but she loves me. After so many bad ones—finally.

(*The Girl enters. She is wearing a T-shirt that says "I am Unlimited" and heavy black eyeliner.*)

### GIRL
Sorry I'm late. Hi.

(*The girl kisses Min timidly, then she really kisses Min, passionately.*)

### MIN
How's my girl?

(*The girl kisses Min again.*)

### MIN
Fine, I see. Great T-shirt. Maybe I should get one, too.

GIRL

Our special place.

(*Min takes out drum sticks and taps out and "sings" "Here Comes the Bride."*)

MIN

Da-dun-du-da. Da-dun-du-da.

GIRL

Oh, Willow, test me again.

MIN

Now?

(*The Girl "nods"*)

MIN

Alright.

(Min taps out sixteenth notes.)

MIN

One eanda. Two eanda. Three eanda.

GIRL

Sixteenth notes.

MIN

Good! And ...

(*Min taps quarter note triplets, slower.*)

MIN

Dah-du-duh. Da-du-duh.

GIRL

Eighth notes.

MIN

Press the reset button.

(*Min taps out quarter note triplets again.*)

MIN

Dah-du-dah. Dah-du-dah.

GIRL

Quarter notes?

MIN

Almost there.

GIRL

Dah-dah-dah--still sounds like quarter notes to me.

MIN

Quarter note triplets.

GIRL

Close enough! A new birthday for me and the best drummer in town. Weeeee!

(*Girl lifts her shirt and shows Min her breasts.*)

MIN

Hey, for my eyes only.

(*Girl pulls her shirt down.*)

MIN

That's better ... W-w-will you marry me?

GIRL

Am I better?

MIN

What? Did you hear what I just said?

GIRL

Yes, yes, but my drumming. Am I better?

MIN

Of course. Yeah.

GIRL

I'm so happy, Minnie.

MIN

You pick out the ring. I didn't know what to get.

GIRL

Now?

MIN

Whenever you want. Got what you want?

GIRL

Yes, yes. No. Maybe.

MIN

Why did you call me Minnie?

(*Min notices someone standing in the distance.*)

MIN

Who's that ? Who is that? Standing behind the tree? Do you know her?

GIRL

Him.

MIN

Him. Him who?

GIRL

Him your nephew.

MIN

Sandro?

GIRL

He dropped by today.

MIN

What timing he's got! I didn't recognize the Jesus look. Hello girly locks. Sandro! San, come over here. You'll be our best man. Why did he run away?

GIRL

He'll be back. He doesn't stutter anymore.

MIN

No?

(*Girl shakes "no."*)

MIN

So he's not stuttering anymore?

                    GIRL
Uh-uh.

                    MIN
How'd that happen?

                    GIRL
We been hanging out. Playing music.
Talking . . . You know, like that.

                    MIN
Like that. Hey. Wow. That's great.

                    GIRL
We're gonna form a band together.

                    MIN
I always said you should. I bet my brother's happy.
Me, too. Me, too. I'm happy, too. Sandro not stut-
tering. Great. And a band.

                    GIRL
Sandro and I—

                    MIN
Wait. Let me guess. Sandro and you—Now that
you've become Sonny and Cher, are no longer
playing Minecraft together.

                    GIRL
Who? (*Beat*) Sometimes we do, but—

                    MIN
And he tried the sex cure? And, oh God.

GIRL

I'm sorry, Min.

MIN

Min.

GIRL

Everybody—

MIN
FOR HOW LONG?

GIRL
I thought maybe we—you and me—I can be a good friend to you.

MIN
But not my wife? (*Beat*) For how long?

GIRL
I don't know. A week.

MIN
A week? That's when you gave me the ultimatum for marriage.

GIRL
It was the day after my drum lesson. But I meant it at the moment. (*Beat*) But San—Sandro's so cute, like a baby male you.

MIN
And where? Where did you hook up?

GIRL

It's not like that, Min.

MIN

Call me Willow.

GIRL

If you don't want to be friends, it's fine . . . Min-
-everybody calls you that. . . I can't say Willow
anymore.

MIN

Shrunken again. A tiny little dot. I made a decision!

GIRL

I love you, but my body—I don't know.

MIN

So when my brother and his wife weren't home, I
hope? He's my nephew, oh God, my brother, sleep-
ing while you—you mixed up little bottom feeder.

GIRL

And who are you? Another person can't be your
breathing machine.

MIN

You chased me. Reeled me in. I taught you things!

GIRL

I taught you things!

MIN

Eyeliner? You're nineteen.

GIRL

I'm sorry, but things change.

MIN

Is that your game?

GIRL

Game?

MIN

Call him. Tell him it's over.

GIRL

I can't do that.

MIN

You're toast. The two of you. Dial. Now.

GIRL

He forgot his cell phone in his locker.

MIN

I'll call him myself.

(*Min dials, but loses the call. She dials again and gets Sandro's voice mail, which is full. Min hangs up.*)

GIRL

See?

MIN

Look, I need you. You need me. I burned every bridge to be with you.

GIRL

Bridges are rebuilt.

MIN

Listen, I read a book on polyamory. We can marry and you can have your candy cane and suck it, too.

GIRL

That's like—like incest.

MIN

This is weird. I always knew it was weird. From the beginning. That note . . . my friends warned me. But I fell . . . hard. Love, why does it always elude me? Now to hear the tsk, tsk, tsk. Whispers and snickers.

GIRL

Screw your hater friends and their ageism.

MIN

I'm an old fool, still hoping. When will I learn?

GIRL

I do love you! Okay, I'll prove it. I accept.

MIN

Accept what?

GIRL

Your proposal. To marry me. What's right is right.

MIN

For real? No reservations?

GIRL

Yes!

MIN

What about—

GIRL

I love you! I love Sandro! I love the whole world!

MIN

Unlimited?

GIRL

It's the totality of possibilities.

MIN

And that means ... Uhh.

GIRL

We all live in the same neighborhood. We can spend holidays together. Have dinner. Walk the dog. Never be alone.

MIN

We don't have a dog.

GIRL

We can get one. Don't be so afraid.

MIN

He's my nephew. I couldn't anyway.

GIRL

This is what I mean about you. Wishy-washy Min.

MIN

Hey!

GIRL

(*taunting*)

Wishy-Washy Min. Wishy-Washy Min. Wishy-
Washy Min.

MIN

(*overlapping*)

D-d-d-don't s-s-s-say-say that. Shut u-u-u up!

GIRL

You sh-sh-shut up!

(*Min washes off her eyeliner with her own spit and stares hard at the
Girl.*)

MIN

See this?

GIRL

Yeah.

MIN

Fuck you and your Maybelline.

(*The girl leaves.*)

MIN

There are limits or people get hurt.

(*She faces audience.*)

## MIN

It's all okay. It's fine. Really fine. I like it here.
Alone. Chewing on the insects and bugs. Alone.
Without my girlfriend, I'm a blank . . . so what's
next? Easy. Take out one nail and replace it with
another nail. Next time, I just got to watch out for
the rust. . . . until then I'll hammer the shit out of
it . . . (*Min gets her drum sticks from her bag.*) One-
eanda-Two-eanda--Three-eanda-Four-eanda . . .

(*Min is playing great. Her timing is perfect. She switches tempos with
precision. She plays faster and faster. But, then, suddenly, when the
tension builds, she starts losing her rhythm, her techniques.*)

## MIN

One—eanda—Two-eanda Three-eanda—Three—
eanda—eanda—YAH. Uhhhh . . . What the—?

(*She tries again, gets it, then loses it, until she has trouble holding the
sticks. She drops them. Picks them up. Drops them again. Picks them up.
Drops them again. She kicks them in frustration. Min faces the audience.*)

## MIN

Wilhelmina Isabel Brewster. Year zero.

(*Min picks up her drum sticks, dusts them off, and leaves.*)

## END OF PLAY

*Words and Music by Angela Costa
Copywight 1996 Angelize Music, Ltd.
Planet records, U.K.
Available on Itunes.

# ACKNOWLEDGMENTS

First, a very special thank you to Donna deMatteo,* without whom the productions of these plays and this book would not have happened.

Special thank-you to: Rosemary DeAngelis, Karen Ludwig, Craig Lucas, Jack Hofsiss, Honor Molloy, Joseph Goodrich, Annie Rachele Lanzillotto, Maria Lisella, Ruthann Robson, Marlene Mancini, Nikolay Sviridchik, Alexander Bartinieff, A.J. Dobbs, Georgia Buchanan, Daniel Nelson, Brian Kafel, Alexis Ortiz, Emma Steen, George Port, Elisa Nieto, Sarah Nochenson, Kate Pressman, Corrie Beth Shotwell, A.C. Davidson, Catherine Siracusa, K.C. Trommer, Lenora Champagne, Elise Teran, Tara Webb, Mike Dobbins, Sara Emily Kuntz, Joan Murray, Edith Meeks, Eric Rasmussen, Mark St. Germain, Laura Shaine Cunningham, Laura Nyro, Angela J. Costa, Nydia Mata, Angelo Primamore, JoAnne Primamore, Michael Primamore, Carol Fox, Etta Seigel, Ellen Goldstein, Little Gray, Barb Pfanz, Jennifer Badamo, Giovani Villari, Grace Grieco, Nicholas Grieco, Esq., Marie Cacciarelli, Sandra Scoppettone, Linda Crawford, Angelina Fiordellisi, and to anyone I might have inadvertently omitted.

*Executive Director of the HB Ten Minute Play Festivals and a member of the Board of HB Studio and HB Playwrights Foundation.

**ELIZABETH PRIMAMORE** studied playwriting at HB Studio. Just Fine and Blank have been produced in HB's Short Play Festivals. Just Fine was published in *Literature and Gender* (Longman, 2011) and *New America* (Autumn House Press, 2012). Craig Lucas and Jack Hofsiss provided dramaturgical support for her full-length play, *Undone,** which has received readings at The Flea, The Cherry Lane, and Ensemble Studio Theatre. *Our First Christmas* and *A Child's Best Interest* have been included in a number of play festivals. She is a fellow at The Virginia Center for the Creative Arts and The Woodstock Byrdcliffe Guild. Her most recent play, *The Professor and Michael Field,* was a semifinalist for the Eugene O'Neill National Playwrights Conference. Elizabeth lives in New York.

*\*Undone* is the fully expanded version of the short play, *Just Fine.*